# The Rescue Princesses
## The Silver Locket

The men ran faster. Rosalind rushed to the gate with the other princesses close behind her. Her heart ached for the little puppy. How could the man treat him so roughly? If only she'd got hold of him quicker...

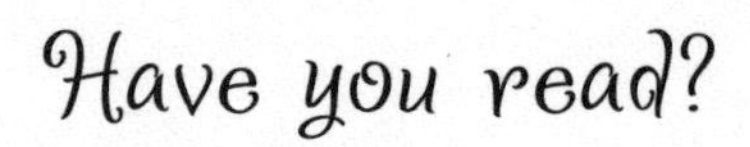

## Have you read?

**The Secret Promise**

**The Wishing Pearl**

**The Moonlit Mystery**

**The Stolen Crystals**

**The Snow Jewel**

**The Magic Rings**

**The Lost Gold**

**The Shimmering Stone**

## Look out for:

**The Ice Diamond**

# The Rescue Princesses
## The Silver Locket

Paula Harrison

nosy crow

For Lydia, Lauren,

Amy, Annabel and Megan

First published in the UK in 2013 by Nosy Crow Ltd
The Crow's Nest, 10a Lant Street
London, SE1 1QR, UK



3 5 7 9 10 8 6 4 2

A CIP catalogue record for this book is available from the British Library



Printed and bound in the UK by Clays Ltd, St Ives Plc

Papers used by Nosy Crow are made from wood grown in sustainable forests.

ISBN: 978 0 85763 191 6

www.nosycrow.com

## Chapter One

# The Land of the Soaring Eagle

Princess Rosalind carefully raked the red and gold leaves into a large heap on the grass. Then she stopped to lean on the end of her rake and gaze up at the mountains. The cold autumn air had turned her cheeks rosy and her blonde hair gleamed in the sunshine. Beside her, Princess Lottie carried on raking.

Behind them was an enormous red-brick house with a beautiful clock tower on top of the roof. This was the home of

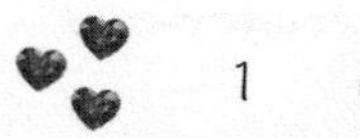

Mr Periwinkle, the famous cookie-factory owner who had invented the greatest cookie of all time – the Chocorama Crunch. He was holding an Autumn Ball and had invited royal families from all around the world to come and stay at his home.

Rosalind was glad to be here in the beautiful country of Taldonia. Although she wished her mum hadn't suggested that they should help out with so many garden jobs. Raking these leaves was taking a very long time!

"Hurry up, Rosalind! There are more leaves over here," called Lottie, pointing her rake at the corner of the garden.

Rosalind stared at Lottie as if she hadn't really heard her. "I'm so glad we came here."

"Me too!" said Lottie. "It's great being together as Rescue Princesses again! It

seems so long since we saw each other."

Rosalind, Lottie, Amina and Isabella had become friends when they'd first met in the springtime. Lottie had told them all about her older sister's adventures and how she and her friends had saved animals from terrible danger. They had been so excited by this idea that they had formed their own secret club and called themselves the Rescue Princesses.

"I'm glad we're together too," Rosalind told Lottie. "But it's not just that! This really feels like the right place to look. I think it's because of those mountains over there."

"Right place to look for what?" Lottie went back to raking furiously, making the leaves fly up and drift down again like multicoloured stars.

Rosalind frowned. "You know! The lost *Book of Ninja*! The note told us to go to

the land of the soaring eagle." She took a piece of paper from her pocket and waved it at Lottie.

"Just imagine!" she added. "The book has every single ninja move inside it. If we can find it we'll learn so much!"

On their last adventure at Amina's palace in the Kingdom of Kamala, the princesses had found a mysterious note that told them to look for a lost book called the *Book of Ninja*. Along with the note they had also found a beautiful necklace with a silver locket, which opened up to reveal a tiny key. Rosalind, who loved mysteries, had been wearing the locket ever since and was longing to go and look for more clues.

"Oh! You're talking about that book again." Lottie shook back her red curls. "Listen, Rosy, I know you really want to find it, but there will be lots of other fun

things to do here!"

"Finding the lost *Book of Ninja* IS fun!" said Rosalind crossly. "And don't call me Rosy. I don't like it!"

Lottie made a face. "Sorry, Ros-a-lind! Oh look, here are the others!"

The bell inside the clock tower gave a loud chime just as two more princesses came running across the grass. Isabella had long brown curls and sparkling eyes. Amina's black hair hung over her shoulders and she smiled shyly at the other girls. They were each carrying an empty basket.

"Guess what!" said Isabella. "We've found out something amazing! You'll never guess what it is."

"Have you found the *Book of Ninja*?" Rosalind's eyes lit up.

"No, that's not it!" said Isabella.

"Have you found an animal that needs

rescuing?" asked Lottie hopefully.

"No, that's not it either!" Isabella turned to Amina. "Shall we make them guess some more or just tell them?"

"Just tell them, I think," said Amina.

Isabella grinned. "One of the princes told us that Mr Periwinkle has a puppy!"

"Aw! Do you think he'd let us play with it?" said Lottie eagerly.

"Maybe he would if he knew we'd finished raking the leaves and collecting the fallen apples," Amina said.

"Let's finish the jobs as quickly as we can!" Isabella spun round so fast that she tripped over the neat pile of leaves Rosalind had made, sending them flying all over the place.

"Isabella!" groaned Rosalind. "It took me ages to rake all those together—" She broke off and stared at the sky over Isabella's shoulder.

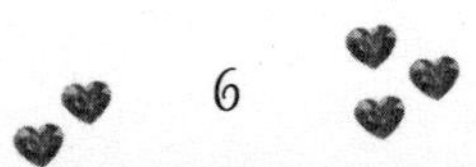

"What's the matter?" Isabella twisted round, trying to see what Rosalind was staring at.

"It must be!" breathed Rosalind. "Look up there – I think that bird is an eagle!"

The princesses gazed at the dark-winged bird soaring gracefully over the tallest mountain peak.

"Are you sure?" said Lottie doubtfully. "Do they even have eagles here in Taldonia?"

"I bet they do! See those wings! The edges look just like fingertips," said Rosalind. "The pictures of eagles I've seen in books look just the same."

A young man wearing green boots and a cap came down the path pushing a wheelbarrow. "Let's ask this gardener!" Isabella rushed over to him. "Excuse me!"

The man stopped when he heard her. He set the wheelbarrow down and

straightened his cap. "Yes, miss. Do you need any help with the raking?"

"No, thank you! We're happy doing it ourselves," beamed Isabella. "We just wondered if you knew what that bird is." She pointed up at the cloudless blue sky.

"That's an eagle, miss – probably a golden eagle by the look of its feathers," he said. "They have a wide wingspan and they love the rocky mountainsides. They're rare, but you do see them now and then flying over the slopes of the Pine Ridge Mountains. Well, I must get on." He picked up his wheelbarrow and carried on down the path.

"You see!" Rosalind burst out. "This is it. *This* is the land of the soaring eagle!"

"I think you're right," said Isabella. "We might find a clue to where the lost book is. What did the note say again?"

Rosalind pulled out the note and read

it carefully. "*I am the* Book of Ninja. *I have been moved to keep my secrets safe from those who would not use them wisely. Follow me to the land of the soaring eagle. Spend time looking and I will open my pages.*"

There was a moment of silence while all the princesses thought about what this meant.

"Even if we are in the right country, that note still doesn't help us much," said Lottie grumpily. "'*Spend time looking*' – that doesn't even tell us where to start!"

"But those soaring eagles could be a clue that it's somewhere nearby," said Isabella. "I think we should begin by looking here in Mr Periwinkle's house."

"Are you wearing the locket, Rosalind?" asked Amina quietly. "I'd like to see it again."

"Yes, it's here!" Rosalind pulled out the necklace from underneath her coat and

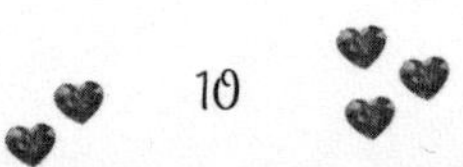

showed them the old-fashioned locket hanging from the silver chain. Engraved on the oval shape was a bird with wide wings.

"The bird on the front looks the same as the eagle we just saw!" said Isabella. "I think we're one step closer to solving the mystery."

Rosalind opened the locket to reveal the tiny silver key inside. "We still don't know what this key is for. But maybe when we work that out, we'll find the *Book of Ninja*!"

## Chapter Two

# The Book Hunt

Rosalind closed the silver locket. "Let's quickly finish tidying the leaves and collecting the apples like we promised. Then we can see the little puppy *and* search the house for clues."

The princesses raced all over the garden, raking leaves and gathering apples into baskets. As soon as they'd finished, Rosalind led the way through the front door into the enormous hallway. A patterned rug lay across the wooden

floor and the walls were dotted with photographs of mountains and forests. Rows of open doors lined the hallway on both sides. A man in a smart uniform wheeled a trolley loaded with cups and muffins past them into a large drawing room. From inside came the murmur of grown-up voices.

Rosalind looked at all the doorways. "Where shall we look first? Do you think the *Book of Ninja* could be on one of the bookshelves?"

"I doubt it. It wouldn't be much of a mystery if it was just standing on a bookshelf," said Lottie.

Rosalind frowned. "I think we should still check them. Maybe there's a bookcase with a glass door that the little key will unlock. We can look for secret hidey-holes too!"

"As long as the grown-ups don't start

wondering what we're doing." Amina twisted a lock of black hair nervously round her finger.

"We'll have to think of something to say in case they see us searching," said Isabella. "We could tell them we're on a pretend treasure hunt."

"If we use ninja moves properly, they won't even notice us," said Rosalind.

So the princesses searched the downstairs rooms. They sneaked around the kings and queens who were drinking coffee in the large drawing room. They crept past a pair of princes doing a jigsaw at a table and tiptoed past a baby sleeping in a pram.

Excitedly they peeked in cupboards and drawers, and even hunted under sofa cushions. They hardly made any noise, apart from when Isabella passed the pram a second time and bumped right

into it, nearly waking up the baby. At last they finished searching the whole ground floor and met up in the hallway again.

"I think we're getting quite good at ninja moves," said Lottie, opening a broom cupboard to check inside.

"We'd get even better if we could find the book," said Rosalind.

"Well, the note says '*Spend time looking*'," said Isabella. "So I guess we just have to keep going."

The door to the large drawing room opened and Rosalind heard her mum's voice. "It's so lovely of you to invite us all to stay, Albert. Do you need any help? Perhaps I could ask the princesses to set the dining table for dinner?"

Rosalind pulled a face. "Let's go upstairs before my mum finds us more jobs to do!" She tiptoed up the stairs, hoping that they didn't creak.

The others followed her and at the top they all crouched down and watched through the banisters as Rosalind's mum swept down the hallway into the garden.

"That's another reason we need the *Book of Ninja*!" said Rosalind. "As well as making us better at rescuing animals, just think of all the horrible royal duties we could avoid with some new ninja moves."

They heard voices again. "That could be my mum coming back – quick!" Rosalind pulled open the nearest door. They dived inside and Lottie shut the door behind them.

They were in a cosy sitting room with two soft brown armchairs and a coffee table. A fire crackled in a small fireplace and the golden flames sent light dancing across the walls. A large wooden bookcase stood in one corner.

"Books!" Rosalind dashed over to the

bookcase, hoping to spot the *Book of Ninja*.

"Shh!" warned Lottie. "Not so loud or the grown-ups will come in and find us."

Rosalind hardly noticed what Lottie was saying. "Where will it be? If the books are in alphabetical order then it could be under N for ninja." She scanned the shelves, trying to work out if the books were in order. She traced a finger along the spine of a book called *A History of Baking*. Where was the lost *Book of Ninja*? She was sure it would look really old and special in some way.

She climbed up on a little stool to look at the highest shelf and pulled out a book with a cheerful yellow cover. The picture on the front showed a pile of delicious-looking biscuits. It was called *Cookies Fit for a King or Queen*. It sounded wonderful but it wasn't what she was looking for.

"Can you see any books that look old?" she asked the others.

There was no reply.

Looking over her shoulder, Rosalind noticed that the other princesses weren't searching the bookcase at all. They were crouched down on the rug next to the coffee table.

"I thought we were finding the lost *Book of Ninja* together!" Rosalind put her hands on her hips. "Why aren't you helping?"

"Oh, Rosalind, come and see!" cried Isabella. "He's so lovely!"

"What's going on?" None of her friends replied so Rosalind jumped down off the stool and went over.

The fire burned cheerfully behind a copper fireguard. As Rosalind got closer, she realised there was something hidden from view behind the coffee table. It

was a large red and blue doggie bed, and inside it was a cute little puppy fast asleep. He lay on his back with his paws curled over. His tummy looked beautifully soft.

As Rosalind knelt down, he woke up and gave a little yawn. He had long floppy ears, a light-brown coat and a dark patch over one eye. Rosalind couldn't help stroking his soft ears.

"Hello, boy. You're lovely, aren't you?" she said gently. "What's your name?"

The puppy barked softly and licked her hand.

The door swung open and Mr Periwinkle came in wearing a stripy purple waistcoat and an emerald-green bowtie. His glasses perched on his nose and a beaming smile lit up his round face. "Hello, young ladies!" he said. "I see you've found my new puppy."

# Chapter Three

# Patch's First Adventure

"I've been keeping him in this room because it's so quiet and cosy." Mr Periwinkle smiled at the princesses. "The fireguard keeps him safely away from the fire, of course."

"What's his name?" asked Amina shyly.

"He's called Patch," said Mr Periwinkle. "It was the first name that came into my head."

"That's a lovely name. It suits him perfectly!" exclaimed Rosalind, stroking Patch's floppy ears again. The little

puppy licked her hand and his stubby tail started wagging.

"Would you like to take him out into the garden?" said Mr Periwinkle. "It'll be the first time that he's gone outside to play. He's not allowed out into the fields or woods yet because he's so little. But I'm sure he'll be fine in the garden with you four princesses looking after him."

"That would be great!" cried Lottie.

"Did you hear that, Patch?" said Isabella. "Would you like to play outside?"

Patch barked and sprang on to her knee, making everyone laugh.

Rosalind looked longingly at the bookcase. What if she had been about to discover the *Book of Ninja* before Mr Periwinkle came in? She just needed a little more time to search for it.

Lottie noticed where she was looking.

"Come on, Rosy! Let's take Patch into the garden. He'll love it out there!"

Mr Periwinkle stood looking at them all and smiling, so Rosalind had no choice but to lift the puppy up and follow the others to the door. She gave the bookcase one last glance before she walked downstairs with her friends.

"Are you all right?" Amina asked her.

Rosalind nodded. "But I'd like another look at that bookcase. There might be another clue. I'm going back there to search again."

Lottie raced past them, calling back, "Hurry up, slowcoaches! There'll be time to search for that old book later!"

Rosalind frowned. She couldn't help thinking that Lottie wasn't taking the look for the *Book of Ninja* very seriously.

Patch wagged his tail and squirmed in Rosalind's arms as she walked out of

the front door into the sunshine. She put him down on the grass and smiled to see him running over the grass and sniffing everything around him.

"Patch, fetch this!" Lottie threw him a red ball that she'd found near the front door. The ball bounced over the grass and the puppy bounded after it. Then Amina caught the ball and threw it for him again.

"My turn!" Isabella caught the ball and swung her arm really high, ready to toss it into the air.

"Don't throw it too hard," said Rosalind. "Patch won't like it – he's only little, remember."

"Don't worry!" said Isabella. "It'll be fine!" But she swung her arm wildly as she let go.

The little red ball went flying towards the house and for a moment Rosalind

thought it would hit a window and smash the glass. But it curled downwards at the last minute and Patch dashed across the garden to get it.

Just as he got close to the ball, it bounced and bashed into a garden rake that was leaning up against the wall. The rake wobbled and fell over, nearly hitting Patch on the nose. He gave a yelp and leapt backwards. The rake landed on the grass in front of him, and he turned and ran away with his tail between his legs.

The princesses sprang forward.

"It's all right, Patch!" called Rosalind. "Come back!"

"Oh dear!" cried Isabella, grabbing the rake and standing it up again. "That scared him, the poor little thing!"

"Where did he go?" said Lottie. "I can't see him anywhere."

Rosalind spun round. Where had Patch

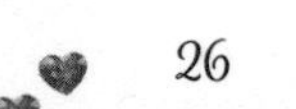

gone? He couldn't have run inside the house because the front door was shut.

"Patch? Where are you?" called Amina softly.

The princesses spread out, looking all around the garden. Rosalind looked behind plant pots and watering cans. She felt sure the little puppy was hiding somewhere.

"Has anyone found him?" called Lottie, and the others shook their heads.

"What will Mr Periwinkle say?" Amina said worriedly. "It was Patch's first time in the garden and we've lost him!"

Isabella's shoulders drooped. "It was all my fault for throwing the ball so hard."

"It was just an accident," said Lottie. "Anyway, we're not going to stop looking until we find him!"

They spread out again. Rosalind paced slowly over the grass, staring hard into

every hiding place. She reached the maple tree on the far side of the garden. Had something moved over here? She stopped and listened.

There was a tiny rustling sound near her feet. On the ground near the tree trunk lay a large pile of leaves. She remembered raking them up earlier that morning. The leaves in the middle of the heap were wobbling.

Rosalind knelt down next to the leaf pile and whispered, "Patch, is that you?"

A little puppy face with a patch over one eye popped out of the middle of the leaves.

Rosalind's heart leapt. "You funny little thing! We were worried about you!"

"Woof! Woof!" barked Patch.

"You found him!" cried Isabella, running over.

Rosalind brushed some fallen leaves off

Patch's head. Then she lifted him into her arms and stroked his soft coat.

"He doesn't look hurt but let's take him back inside where it's warm, just to be sure," said Lottie.

"He might not have been all right if I hadn't found him," said Rosalind.

"I'm sorry I knocked the rake over," said Isabella. "But look – he's fine now."

"Puppies need careful looking after," said Rosalind. "It was lucky that the rake didn't hit him—"

"Isabella's said she's sorry," Lottie interrupted. "So don't keep going on about it."

"I wasn't!" said Rosalind. "I just meant we should be more careful with Patch."

Isabella sniffed and ran inside.

"Oh no! She's upset now!" said Amina, and ran after her.

Rosalind hurried towards the house, but

Lottie caught up with her as she reached the front door. "Just leave Isabella alone for a while," she told Rosalind. "Honestly, Rosy! How can we be Rescue Princesses together when you're being so cross?" Then she went inside and shut the door behind her.

Rosalind sighed and rubbed her cheek against Patch's coat. "Oh, Patch! I didn't mean it like that. Sometimes the things I say just come out wrong." She blinked back a tear and Patch licked her cheek.

"Thank you, Patch! I wish it was as easy to be friends with the other princesses as it is with you. And I really wish Lottie would stop calling me Rosy!"

## Chapter Four

# The Princess and the Puppy

After his adventure in the leaf pile, Patch snuggled up in Rosalind's arms. He seemed happy, so she took him back inside. His eyes stayed open all the way up the stairs, looking at everything around him.

The fire was still burning cheerfully in the little room with the bookcase. Rosalind knelt down and laid Patch gently inside his doggie bed.

"There! Now you'll be warm and

comfy," she said.

Patch snuffled at the soft bed and then yawned widely.

"If the others aren't helping, then we'll have to look for the *Book of Ninja* by ourselves, won't we?" added Rosalind.

Patch gave a short bark as if he agreed.

Rosalind returned to the bookcase and checked along every shelf. There was nothing called the *Book of Ninja,* but that just made her even more determined. After all, she hadn't expected it to be easy. The note said: *'Spend time looking and I will open my pages'*. Maybe if she searched for long enough, she would stumble upon the book somehow.

Perhaps there were more books somewhere else. This was a big house, so there were plenty of places to look.

"You stay there and sleep, Patch. I'll come back and see you later." She kissed

the top of the puppy's head and went out into the passageway.

Her sapphire ring gleamed on her finger. It was such a beautiful deep-blue colour. It made her remember how happy she and the other Rescue Princesses had been the first time their rings had worked. They each had a magic ring made from a different jewel. Hers was a sapphire, Amina's was an emerald, Lottie's was a ruby and Isabella's a yellow topaz. They used these jewels to call each other for help, especially if there was an animal in danger.

She hadn't realised till now how much she had liked being able to speak to the others if she needed to. It felt strange to be going on an adventure by herself.

Creeping down the corridor, she listened carefully outside each door before opening it and looking inside.

Then she looked in cupboards and on shelves for more books, until she had searched every room on that floor.

Just as she was about to climb the stairs to the top floor, she heard footsteps coming down. She shrank back into a window alcove and curled the red velvet curtain around her shoulders to hide her.

A scuffling movement by her feet made her jump. It was Patch. He must have followed her from the sitting room.

She picked him up and held him tight just as a queen wearing a long purple dress swept by. The queen didn't notice the bulging curtain and carried on down the stairs. Rosalind breathed out slowly. Patch snuffled at her shoulder and gave a little whine.

"Shh!" she giggled. "What is it? Do you want to come on an adventure too?"

Patch wagged his tail.

"All right then! But you have to be really quiet, OK? Like a ninja dog!" She carried him upstairs, grinning to herself at the thought of Patch doing ninja moves.

She reached the top of the stairs and stopped outside the first room. Her hand froze on the door handle. There were girls talking inside. She leaned a little closer. She recognised those voices.

"My sister, Emily, gave me some more jewels to bring along. Some of them already have a magic power." Lottie's voice rang out like a bell.

"That's fantastic!" said Amina. "But don't you think we should go and find Rosalind so that she can join in too? We've always done everything together – the four of us. It feels strange without her."

Rosalind had to bend really close to

the door to be able to hear Amina's soft voice. Her fingers tightened on the door handle. She was glad that Amina missed her!

"You're right!" said Lottie. "Rosalind needs to see these jewels too. Are you ready to go and look for her, Isabella?"

"Of course!" said Isabella. "Poor Patch! I didn't mean to knock the rake over and scare him. I feel awful about the whole thing."

Rosalind's cheeks flushed. She hadn't meant to make Isabella feel bad. She turned the handle and burst into the room. "It's all right, Isabella! Patch is absolutely fine! Look – he's really happy." She held Patch up to show them and he wagged his tail extra hard.

Isabella smiled. "We were just coming to look for you. Where've you been?"

Rosalind sat down on the bed next to

Isabella and gave her Patch to cuddle. "I've been looking for the *Book of Ninja*, but it's not half as much fun searching on my own. I really am sorry about what I said before, Isabella."

"That's OK!" Isabella stroked Patch's velvety ears. "I'm glad you're here. You have to see these new jewels that Lottie brought along. They look amazing."

Lottie carried over a large golden box, which had a row of small jewel-making tools inside. When she pulled out a hidden drawer at the bottom, Rosalind saw a heap of jewels that glittered in every colour, from bright, clear diamonds to deep-red rubies.

"Look at this!" Lottie picked out a bracelet that shone with a dazzling green light. "They're emeralds that light up just like a torch. My sister told me that Princess Jaminta made it. She's the one

who crafted the very first Rescue Princess magical jewels!"

"Wow!" Rosalind stared at the glowing emeralds on the bracelet. "That's so bright! Maybe we could use it when we search for the *Book of Ninja*."

Lottie frowned. "Is there much point in spending all our free time searching for that book? We haven't had any luck so far. We don't even have any clues."

"But the note says: *'Spend time looking'*." Rosalind got the note out of her pocket again and tried to give it to Lottie. "So we *have* to spend the time!"

Lottie waved the piece of paper away. "I know it does! But how does that help us? The book could be anywhere!"

*Bong!* The loud chime made the girls jump.

Isabella giggled. "Oh, that happened before. I think my room must be just

underneath that clock tower. It's loud, isn't it?"

"At least you won't forget the time and be late for dinner," said Amina, smiling.

"No, I won't forget the . . ." Isabella paused. "That's funny!"

"What is?" asked Lottie.

"Just now we were saying we should *spend time* searching for the book. Then the clock chimed and Amina said I wouldn't *forget time*," Isabella explained. "It made me think about the note from the locket again."

Rosalind unfolded the note and read it once more. Then she went to Isabella's window and opened it. "The clock tower is right above you." She stuck her head out of the window and craned upwards. She could see the hands of the clock above her, gleaming in the sunshine.

"I don't understand," said Amina.

"What does the clock have to do with the silver locket and the note?"

Rosalind drew her head back in. Her cheeks glowed with excitement. "Maybe the bit about spending time *is* a clue! Maybe that's where we should be looking."

"You mean: clocks tell us the time . . . so that's where the book could be hidden?" said Isabella.

"Exactly!" Rosalind grinned. "The note says *Spend time looking,* and the clock is the thing that gives us the time!"

"You could be right." Lottie's eyes gleamed. "'*Spend time looking*' . . . it didn't really sound like a clue at first, but it would make sense. Is there a way to get up to the clock tower?"

"There's a little spiral staircase right at the end of the corridor," said Amina. "I haven't gone up there, but it could lead

to the tower."

Sensing their excitement, Patch wriggled out of Isabella's arms, romped across her bed and jumped on to the pillow. Then he turned round and dashed all the way back again.

Rosalind took a deep breath. "Will you come with me? I want us to go and look together, like proper Rescue Princesses."

"Are you crazy?" said Lottie. "Of course we're coming!"

Amina smiled and added, "We wouldn't miss it for the world."

## Chapter Five

# The Mysterious Clock Tower

Rosalind closed the jewel box and hid it in a drawer. Lottie slipped the emerald bracelet on to her wrist, hiding it under her long sleeve so that no one would see it. Then the princesses pelted down the corridor with Patch galloping behind them.

"It's here!" Amina showed them the little wooden staircase that curled upwards. "I knew it must lead to the very top of the house."

Rosalind picked up Patch and they all climbed the spiral staircase, their footsteps drumming on the wooden steps. A dusty square window halfway up gave them a good view of the garden below. It was dark at the top so Lottie got out the emerald bracelet, which cast an eerie green light over the walls.

Rosalind tucked Patch under one arm and looked around. They were in a long, narrow passageway. "We have to go this way. The other way is a dead end."

As they walked on, Lottie held up her arm to light the way with the emeralds. After a few steps Rosalind banged her head and stopped, making Lottie bump into her.

"Don't stop suddenly like that!" Lottie grumbled.

"Sorry! It's just that the ceiling's low here and I banged my head," Rosalind

told her. "Crouch down a bit, everyone, or you'll bump your heads too."

They carried on, bending their heads, until they came out into a small, bare room with wooden floorboards. Light streamed down from a window in the sloping roof. A steady ticking noise came from the wall on one side. All the princesses rushed towards it.

"There's a tiny door in the wall." Amina pointed at a small wooden door with a silver keyhole.

"That must be how they reach the machinery behind the clock if they need to mend it," said Lottie. "But we haven't got a key."

"Oh yes we have!" Rosalind set Patch down and opened the silver locket on the chain around her neck. She took out the tiny key and fitted it into the lock.

"Go on, Rosalind! Open it!" said

Isabella breathlessly.

Rosalind turned the key and the little wooden door swung open. Inside was a mass of bronze-coloured cogs and wheels all ticking and turning. The round shape of the clock could be seen on the wall at the far side.

"Where's the book?" said Lottie.

"Here!" Rosalind picked up a large rectangle of red material. She unwrapped the crimson cloth to reveal an old-fashioned black book. The gold lettering on the cover spelled *Book of Ninja*.

"Wow!" said Isabella. "We found it at last. This is so awesome!"

"It looks really old," whispered Amina. "Look at the way some of the pages have turned brown."

Rosalind opened the black cover and gazed at a picture that showed a ninja climbing up a tree to hide. The picture

had labels on, showing how to complete the move successfully. A heading at the top of the page read *Hints and Tips*.

"Look at this!" Lottie turned to a page with the title *How to Spot an Enemy Hiding in a Forest*. "This is amazing!"

The girls crowded round the book, turning over the pages. There was a muffled thump from outside, but they took no notice.

"'Ere we go!" said a man's voice. "Someone's left the window open. Let's see what's inside."

"Hurry up, before they come back," called another man faintly.

Amina clutched Rosalind's wrist. "What's that?"

The princesses looked at each other.

"It sounds like someone's right outside," whispered Isabella. "But they can't be. We're too high up."

"Maybe it's the person in the bedroom below," hissed Lottie.

"Bloomin' difficult . . . climbing through these little windows," grumbled the man.

Rosalind closed the *Book of Ninja*. "He *does* sound as if he's just outside. Let's find out what's going on. There's a window on the staircase. We can look from there."

The girls rushed back along the narrow passage. Amina picked Patch up and followed behind the others. They stopped halfway down the staircase and Rosalind wiped the dusty window with her sleeve.

"There's a ladder leaning up against the wall," said Lottie. "And a man with dark hair and a beard is standing at the bottom."

"Perhaps he's going to fix something or do some painting," Isabella suggested.

Rosalind leaned closer to the window.

"There's another man too," she said. "He's climbing out of a window on to the top of the ladder, right underneath the clock tower. He's holding something. I don't think they're painting." An awful thought popped into her head. "Do you think Mr Periwinkle knows they're here or do you think they're stealing?"

"I hope not!" said Amina. "Whose bedroom is that?"

"I don't think it's mine," said Isabella. "I'm sure I shut my window before we came up here. What shall we do?"

"We need to work out what he's got in his hand and if he took it from that bedroom," said Lottie. "We have to get closer."

The princesses ran down the staircase and along the corridor. Stopping to check that there were no grown-ups nearby, they raced down two more flights of stairs

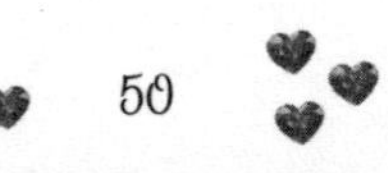

to the hallway.

Amina peeked round the door of the large drawing room. "Most of the grown-ups are in here," she whispered to the others.

"We'd better leave Patch inside as he's so little," Rosalind told her. "Don't let anyone see you though."

Amina tiptoed into the drawing room and placed Patch on an armchair near the door. He looked up at her in surprise from the velvet cushion as she backed away.

"Quick!" Rosalind grabbed Amina's hand and pulled her out of the front door.

"We heard those men's voices when we were inside the clock tower," said Lottie, beckoning them round the corner of the house. "So they must be over here."

They crept along, keeping close to the

wall. Rosalind realised she was holding the *Book of Ninja*, so she tucked it under her arm out of the way. The ladder was a short distance away beyond some bushes. The man with the dark beard was still standing at the foot of the ladder. He glared round, as if he thought someone might be watching.

"Get down!" hissed Isabella, and the girls ducked out of view.

The second man, who was broad-shouldered with a bald head, climbed slowly down from the upstairs window. His heavy frame made the ladder wobble and the bearded man had to hold it steady. At last he stepped off the bottom rung and showed a bundle of stuff to his friend.

"What is he holding?" whispered Rosalind. "I still can't see what it is."

Silently she tiptoed closer and hid

behind a bush a very short distance from the bottom of the ladder.

The bald man was holding a shiny bundle in his cupped hands. Grinning, the bearded man picked something off the top of the pile and held it up. A long golden necklace with an amber jewel gleamed brightly.

Rosalind felt anger bubble inside her. She knew who owned that necklace and these men had no right to take it.

"They must be thieves," said Lottie, creeping up behind her. "They've got a whole bunch of jewellery there."

"That's my mum's favourite necklace," Rosalind told her. "Those men are stealing and they mustn't get away with it!"

## Chapter Six
# Thieves on the Run

"We should go and get Mr Periwinkle," muttered Amina. "Those men are much bigger than us – we need to tell the adults what's happening."

Rosalind stared at the thieves. She knew Amina was right. "OK. We'll fetch the grown-ups, but we need to make sure they don't get away."

The bearded man took all the jewellery from the other man's hands and stuffed it into the pockets of his coat. "Now, get

back up that ladder and into the next room," he said. "If we can get this much stuff from one bedroom, then we'll soon have mountains of jewellery!"

"I'm tired," puffed the other man. "We've got lots here. Why don't we just go?"

"Don't be silly!" snapped the bearded man. "We need more. Look at this gold ring." He held up the shiny golden circle. "There could be something like this in every room. Get back up there."

"What if someone comes?" whined the bald man. "They might send for the police."

"No one will come. The gardener went home and all those rich guests are inside."

The princesses sneaked slowly backwards, keeping down low. Rosalind's heart thumped. They must get back to

the grown-ups without being seen.

The bald man began to climb back up the ladder just as the girls heard a panting sound behind them. Patch galloped round the corner of the house and sprang towards the princesses.

Rosalind tried to catch hold of him. "Patch! Shh!" she hissed.

Patch bounced past her and noticed the two thieves. He froze and his tail stopped wagging. Then he made a low growl.

Lottie and Rosalind both dived towards him, but it was too late. The little puppy sprang out of the bushes, barking at the men as loudly as he could.

The bearded man strode towards Patch, leaving his friend wobbling on the ladder. "Quiet, you little pest!"

"Make it stop yapping!" quavered the bald man, climbing down. "Everyone will come out of the house and see us."

"Silence!" hissed the bearded man, but Patch wouldn't stop. "We'll have to take him with us – the mucky little thing." He grabbed the puppy roughly and bundled him underneath his coat. Then the two men ran across the grass to the garden gate.

Rosalind jumped up, horrified. "You can't take him! He's only a puppy."

The men turned round and saw the girls.

"Stay back!" the bearded man snarled at Rosalind. "Or we'll take that shiny silver locket you're wearing too." Then they ran through the gate and away down the driveway.

"Stop! Burglars!" shouted Lottie, but no one came out of the house.

The men ran faster. Rosalind rushed to the gate with the other girls close behind her. Her heart ached for the little puppy.

How could the man treat him so roughly? If only she'd got hold of him quicker.

"Poor Patch! He must be terrified!" cried Isabella.

"We have to split up," said Lottie quickly. "Rosalind, Isabella! You two follow the men and try to keep track of which way they go. Amina and I will tell the grown-ups about the burglars."

Rosalind dashed through the gate followed by Isabella. "We'll use our rings to tell you where we are," she called back.

The man with the beard had reached the bottom of the sloping gravel drive and instead of heading towards the road he veered right into the woods. The bald man ran behind, struggling to keep up.

Rosalind and Isabella raced down the drive after them. By the time they got to the bottom of the slope, the men had disappeared. The girls ran to the place

where they'd entered the wood.

It was dark under the trees. A branch suddenly creaked just above their heads.

"I don't like it in here," said Isabella.

"I don't either," Rosalind admitted. "But we have to help Patch. I think the men went this way."

The girls hurried through the wood, looking for any sign of the burglars. A twig cracked under Isabella's feet.

"Careful!" murmured Rosalind. "Let's stand still and listen out for the burglars. If they're moving we should hear them."

They stopped and listened hard. The wind blew through the branches, making the red and gold leaves flutter like flags.

"Do you think we should go back?" said Isabella, shivering. "They could be anywhere. They could be waiting for us behind a tree."

"We must keep going and find Patch."

Rosalind thought for a second. She felt something hard underneath her arm and remembered that she was still holding the *Book of Ninja*. "Maybe something in here will help us."

Opening the cover, she flicked to the contents page and scanned the chapter titles. There it was! The section that Lottie had looked at: *How to Spot an Enemy Hiding in a Forest*. It was on page eighty-two. She flicked to the right page. The squiggly letters of the ninja alphabet covered one side and on the opposite page was the translation. At the top was a picture showing a ninja crouching high up in a tree. Rosalind read on:

*Many people believe that it is easy to hide in a forest. But ninja skills can be used to spot an enemy's hiding place.*

*1. Listen for the sounds of the forest, such as birds and insects. Anything different could*

*be your hidden enemy.*

*2. Look for crushed leaves, broken branches and footprints. These are signs that your enemy has passed that way.*

*3. Look for animals and birds disturbed by your enemy's movements. Crows, in particular, are quick to spot people lurking below.*

*ABOVE ALL . . . when moving towards your enemy – use distraction! A cry of fire or the howl of a wolf may flush them from their hiding place.*

Rosalind felt a fizzing in her stomach. She was sure this would work. She turned to the next page, which was headed *Using Camouflage in a Forest* and *Making a Trap in the Forest*. Those things might come in handy later. She closed the book.

"Listen, Isabella!" she said. "Can you hear anything?"

Isabella's eyes widened. "Just the wind

BOOK OF NINJA

in the treetops and a few birds. No, wait!" She turned her head and listened. "There's something else – a squeaky noise."

"I bet that's them," said Rosalind. "Come on!"

They moved stealthily through the wood, placing each foot carefully to avoid stepping on leaves that might rustle or twigs that might crack. Every now and then they paused to listen for the noise. It was such a high, unhappy sound that Rosalind started to wonder if it was Patch whining. Her heart sank. He must be a very frightened little puppy.

"Rosalind!" whispered Isabella. "Look at those birds."

Rosalind followed her gaze. Two crows were sitting together on a tree branch. One flapped its wings and flew away. The other turned its black head as if it

was eyeing something on the ground. It opened its beak and cawed loudly.

"Do you think the thieves have disturbed them, like the *Book of Ninja* says?" said Isabella.

"Maybe." Rosalind stared over at the bushes underneath the tree where the crow perched. "We could be really close. We'd better not move in case they see us."

The princesses crouched down for several minutes. Rosalind's heart thumped so loud she was sure the men would hear it. A prickly bramble scratched her arm and she shifted uncomfortably.

"Do you really think the men are over there?" hissed Isabella.

"I don't know." Rosalind opened the *Book of Ninja* again. She stared at the page on finding an enemy in a forest. The last sentence stood out: *A cry of fire or the*

*howl of a wolf may flush them from their hiding place.*

It was time to use that advice. She took a deep breath and cupped her hands round her mouth, letting out a long and eerie wolf howl.

## Chapter Seven

# The Wolf Howl Trick

As Rosalind finished the long howl, there was an answering yelp. The bushes rustled and the bald man leapt out.

"There's a wolf!" he cried. "We could be eaten!"

"Get down!" A hand reached out from the next bush and yanked him downwards. "There are no wolves living in this part of the country. It's probably just a child mucking about."

Hearts thumping, Rosalind and Isabella

crept backwards until they reached a really good hiding place behind a fallen log. Just as they crouched down behind it, the bald man stood up again and stared all around. "How can you be sure it's not a wolf? I'm sure I heard something coming towards us. What if it's real?"

Patch let out a high whine. "Silence, both of you!" The bearded man rose from his hiding place, his pockets bulging with all the stolen jewellery. "We were *supposed* to be waiting to see if anyone had followed us, you dummy!"

"But nobody saw us," said the bald man. "Oh, except those little girls but they wouldn't dare come after us."

The man with the beard drew Patch from underneath his coat and gave him to the bald man. "There – you have him. I can't stand carrying him any more."

The bald man sighed as he took the

puppy. Patch wriggled unhappily, his tail drooping. Staring suspiciously around, the two men walked away along the forest path.

"Huh!" said Isabella as soon as the men were out of earshot. "So they think the little girls wouldn't dare come after them, do they?"

"They didn't know they were dealing with Rescue Princesses." Rosalind's blue eyes glinted. "We'll show them."

They followed the men by sneaking from tree to tree and ducking down if one of them turned round. At the far edge of the wood the men took a footpath along the side of a field until they came to an old, run-down barn. A fence behind the barn separated the field from an orchard of apple trees.

"I'll get the car," said the bearded man. "Tie up that mutt while I'm gone. I don't

want him getting free." He marched off towards the main road while the bald man went into the barn with Patch.

"Now what shall we do?" whispered Isabella.

"Let's call the others." Rosalind pressed the sapphire in the centre of her ring. The blue jewel lit up brightly, and she lifted her hand and spoke straight into it. "Lottie! Amina! Are you there?"

There was a moment of silence before Lottie's voice came faintly through the ring. "We're here! Have you kept track of the burglars?"

"Yes! We're watching them now. Have you told Mr Periwinkle what happened?"

"He's calling the police," said Lottie. "Where shall we find you?"

"Take the footpath through the wood until you reach a field on the other side. Then turn right and walk along until

you see an old barn," Rosalind told her. "And watch out – these thieves are pretty sneaky."

"We'll be careful," Lottie replied. Then her voice faded and the light inside the sapphire vanished.

A long whine from inside the barn tugged at Rosalind's heart. She was determined to see if Patch was all right. There were slits high up in the barn wall. If she climbed up on something she might be able to see inside.

"I'm going to see if I can look in," she told Isabella.

"OK, but be careful."

Rosalind climbed on to an animal's drinking trough and Isabella helped to steady her. Balancing carefully, Rosalind put her eye to a chink in the wall. She could see the inside of the barn. She leaned closer, trying to get a view of

Patch. He was tied up near the back. The bald man had fastened a piece of old rope to his collar and tied the other end to a wheelbarrow. The little puppy crouched down, his brown eyes wide. He gave another high whimper.

"Stop that!" grumbled the bald-headed thief. "No silly whining!" He lay down on a stack of hay bales and closed his eyes.

Rosalind glared at the man, wishing she could tell him how unkind he was. She reminded herself it was a good thing that he didn't know she was watching. They would need their very best ninja moves to rescue Patch.

"Rosalind!" hissed Isabella. "The others are here."

Rosalind got down from the trough. She could see Lottie's red curls bouncing as she ran across the field. Amina was just behind her.

Rosalind put a finger to her lips and pointed to the barn to show the others that they had to be quiet.

"Did Mr Periwinkle believe you straightaway when you told him about the thieves?" Isabella asked Lottie and Amina.

"He was surprised at first," Lottie whispered back. "Then he saw the ladder and Rosalind's mum realised her jewellery was gone. Then everyone rushed off to check if their things had been taken, while Mr Periwinkle called the police."

"We tried to tell him that we knew where the thieves were, but he didn't hear us," Amina explained. "There was so much noise from everyone trying to talk at once and then the Queen of Hadderland went and fainted."

"We knew we had to help you rescue

Patch, so we sneaked away just before we got your message," said Lottie.

"Everyone, hide!" said Isabella. "The other man's coming back."

They ran behind the barn just as the bearded man marched back up the path.

"What are you doing lying down on the hay like that?" he barked at the bald man. "Hurry up! The car's ready. Bring that puppy too. If we leave him here he might lead someone to the car's tyre tracks and then they could follow us."

"Quick, Rosalind! Do something!" said Isabella urgently. "Once they've got in their car we'll have no chance of rescuing Patch. Do your wolf howl again!"

Amina and Lottie looked at Rosalind in surprise.

"What wolf howl?" asked Amina.

"There's no time to explain. I'll distract them while you sneak round the side."

Rosalind passed the *Book of Ninja* to Amina. Then she ran to the fence that separated the field from the apple orchard. As she climbed up, an apple-tree branch scraped against her neck, but she pushed it away and scrambled over.

With a quick look behind her, she ran further into the orchard. Then, when she was safely hidden behind a large tree, she tipped back her head and let out a long wolf howl.

There was a shout from inside the wooden barn and the thieves came out running.

## Chapter Eight

# Patch's Great Escape

Rosalind finished the wolf call and ducked down. She rubbed her neck. Her skin was sore where the branch had scraped her.

"That's twice we've heard that wolf howl," said the man with the beard. "It can't be an accident. I'm going to find out who's doing this."

Rosalind shrank down behind the tree trunk. She could see the other princesses disappearing round the corner of the

barn. Her friends were going to find Patch and soon he would be safe and free.

"As long as it's not a real wolf. . ." The bald man walked into the middle of the field, shading his eyes with one hand.

"The noise came from over here in this orchard, you fool!" The bearded man marched over to the fence. "Whoever it is, they're probably hiding among these apple trees."

Isabella peeked round the corner of the barn and gave Rosalind a thumbs-up sign behind the thieves' backs. Rosalind grinned. That meant they'd untied Patch. Now all they had to do was get away without the men seeing.

"Wait! What's this!" said the bearded man.

Rosalind wasn't looking at him. She scanned the apple trees around her, working out how to sneak away without

being spotted.

"That looks expensive," said the bald man. "Made of silver . . . and look, there's a little key inside it."

Rosalind froze and her hand went to her neck.

The silver locket was gone.

Her insides felt like jelly as she peered round the tree trunk. The thieves were holding her silver locket. She loved that locket. It had helped them find the *Book of Ninja*.

The bearded man stared at the necklace, his face darkening. "I bet it's all been a trick!"

"What has?" The other man's face creased with confusion. "I don't—"

"I bet those pesky little princesses followed us here," snarled the bearded man. "When I find them they'll be sorry!"

"You mean those princesses we saw in

the garden?" said the bald man. "They wouldn't dare!"

"Don't you remember?" said the other thief. "One of them was wearing a locket that looked just like this."

Round the edge of the trunk, Rosalind could see the other girls tiptoeing out of the barn. Lottie led the way and Isabella held Patch tightly. Amina was still carrying the *Book of Ninja*. Rosalind crossed her fingers, hoping the thieves wouldn't turn round.

She picked up a fallen apple. Maybe there was another way to distract the men. Pulling back her arm, she threw the apple as hard as she could. It went soaring through the air and struck the bald man on the shoulder.

"Ow!" he groaned. "That hurt!"

"That throw was too good for a princess," said the bearded man. "I bet

there's another bunch of thieves that want our loot." He was halfway over the orchard fence when he caught sight of Amina, Lottie and Isabella sneaking along next to the barn wall.

"Oh, look!" The bald man caught sight of them too. "It *is* those princesses."

"I don't believe it!" The bearded man leapt off the fence. "How did you follow us? Well, you won't be going anywhere now – we're not letting you go back to tell tales!" He rushed at the girls but Patch scampered towards him and ran right between his legs.

The burglar grabbed at the little puppy, but Patch bounced out of his way with a bark of delight.

"Careful, Patch! Don't get caught!" cried Rosalind.

Patch woofed happily and dashed round the man's ankles, until the thief

looked quite dizzy.

"Get out of my way, you silly mongrel!" he bellowed, but Patch wouldn't stop. He kept on galloping round and round. The man spun faster and faster as he tried to catch the puppy. At last he lost his balance and toppled over, landing heavily on his bottom. The silver locket flew out of his hands on to the grass.

"Rosalind! Meet us in the wood!" yelled Lottie, pulling Amina and Isabella after her.

"Good boy, Patch!" called Isabella. "Come on, this way!" Patch pricked up his ears and raced after them.

Rosalind dashed from her hiding place and climbed back over the fence. She could see her friends ahead of her, racing away down the footpath with Patch galloping behind.

"'Ere you go!" The bald man tried to

help his friend up.

The bearded man refused his hand with a glare. "I've twisted my ankle, you fool! I can't run. You'll have to catch them yourself. Hurry up before they get away!"

Rosalind dodged past the men, picked up her precious silver locket and fastened it round her neck. Then she ran and ran, hoping that her legs would go fast enough. She caught up with the others in the wood. They were running along a path that wound through the trees back to Mr Periwinkle's house. Amina held the *Book of Ninja* in one hand. Patch ran alongside them.

Rosalind cast a worried look at the bald man lumbering after them. He didn't look fast but his legs were long. What if he caught them? Would he take Patch away again?

"I think he's going to catch us,"

Rosalind called to the others. "We have to do something!"

"Just run faster! We have to get back to the house," shouted Lottie, swinging her arms as she ran. Every time her hand swung down, a ray of green light shone out from underneath her sleeve. It was the bracelet with the glowing emeralds.

An idea flashed into Rosalind's mind. "Wait, Lottie! Pass me your bracelet." She ran alongside Lottie and took the bracelet from her arm.

"What are you doing?" said Lottie. "How is that going to help?"

"I'm not sure yet, but they're the only magical jewels we've got right now!" Rosalind darted behind a wide tree trunk. "Keep going without me!" she told the others. "Tell Mr Periwinkle where the thieves are."

"Don't you think we should stay

together?" said Amina.

"That's right – aren't we safer that way?" Isabella stopped to pick up Patch, who was looking tired.

"No! You've got to go on!" said Rosalind fiercely. "Then at least you can explain to Mr Periwinkle what's happening."

"Good luck!" Amina hugged her before she ran after Lottie and Isabella.

Rosalind watched them go, hiding behind the tree trunk. Then she turned her attention to the emeralds. There had to be a way these jewels would help – some way to use them to slow the thief down.

The man was nearer now. She could hear him panting for breath. She twisted round to check how close he was, her heart thumping. She had to keep the bracelet hidden, otherwise its bright-green light would show him where she was hiding.

That was it! She knew exactly how to use the bracelet. The light from the emeralds would help.

The thief's footsteps thundered on the path and a squirrel leapt away in fright.

Rosalind swallowed. She had to do this now, before the thief passed by. She held out her arm, casting the light from the jewels far and wide, and stepped out from behind the tree.

Chapter Nine

# The Glowing Emeralds

The bald-headed thief stopped a few steps away. "There you are! You won't get away now. . . Hey! What's that you're wearing?"

"They're emeralds. Would you like one?" Rosalind said daringly, and she held out the bracelet. Then as the man lurched forwards she took the bracelet's golden thread and snapped it, letting the dazzling jewels pour into her hand.

"Catch it then!" She threw one emerald

high in the air and it landed on the ground some distance away, still shining brightly.

"Silly girl! That's easy to find." The man groped for the jewel among the autumn leaves.

Rosalind raced away through the trees, pleased that the thief had fallen for her trick.

The bald man picked up the emerald and chased her. Soon he began to catch her up again. Breathlessly she threw another emerald behind her. It went bouncing across the ground and then lay still, like a little forest star.

"I want all of them," howled the thief. "Give me all the jewels!"

Rosalind ran on. She knew the thief wouldn't stop for long. Her feet ached and her legs felt heavy.

"Rosalind!" Amina waved to her from

the edge of the trees.

Rosalind saw Lottie and Isabella waiting there too. "I – can't – run – any – more!" she puffed.

"Watch out!" yelled Lottie.

The man sped up, his feet pounding behind her.

"Quick! Give me those jewels." Lottie took the rest of the emeralds from Rosalind and handed them round. "Let's throw them all over the place!"

Patch barked loudly as the princesses scattered the emeralds everywhere.

The thief wailed and scrambled through bushes and brambles, trying to find all the jewels. Leaving him complaining, the princesses raced out of the wood and up the driveway to the house.

Rosalind's mum came running through the garden gate. "What happened?" she cried. "You're covered in mud and

scratches."

"One of the burglars is down in the wood," Rosalind told her breathlessly. "They took Patch and so we rescued him!"

"It's true!" said Amina, tucking the *Book of Ninja* under her arm where it wouldn't be noticed.

"Rosalind!" cried her mum. "What were you thinking?"

"It's all right. We didn't let them see us," explained Lottie. "Except that they did catch sight of us at the end. Did the police arrive?"

Mr Periwinkle came out of the house talking to a pair of tall policemen. "We think they only stole from one bedroom," he said. "Nothing's missing from any of the other rooms."

"Mr Periwinkle! One of the burglars is in the wood!" cried Rosalind.

"Good gracious! Are you sure?" said Mr Periwinkle.

"We saw him," said Isabella, "when we were rescuing Patch."

The princesses exchanged looks. They knew it was best not to explain too much about the adventure. What they did as Rescue Princesses *was* a secret, after all.

The policemen sprinted down to the wood to find the thief, just as another police car drove up. In the back of the car sat the bearded man with a sulky look on his face.

A policewoman climbed out of the car. "Is this one of the men you saw stealing?" she asked. "We found him by an old barn not far away, with his pockets full of jewellery." She handed the necklaces and rings to Mr Periwinkle.

"That's my jewellery!" cried Rosalind's mum. "Thank goodness you found it."

"Is this one of the men you saw?" Mr Periwinkle asked the girls.

They all nodded. "It's definitely him!" said Lottie firmly.

Patch jumped down from Isabella's arms and gave a little growl. The man with the beard scowled even more.

"Aw, Patch! You look so cute when you do that!" Rosalind bent down to rub the puppy's long velvety ears.

"Bless me! Here's another one!" said Mr Periwinkle, watching the policemen march the bald man up the driveway. "Thank you, officers! And thank you too, girls. It's because of you that we knew about the robbery so quickly!"

"No problem at all!" said Lottie airily. "We're glad to have helped."

"Is there anything I can do to reward you?" asked Mr Periwinkle, smiling.

Rosalind thought hard. Then her

stomach rumbled. "I'd love to try one of your famous biscuits – the Chocorama Crunch!"

"What a good idea!" Mr Periwinkle waved them inside. "Why don't you go in and I'll have some cookies sent upstairs for you with some lemonade."

"Thank you!" The princesses curtsied.

"Could you. . ." Amina flushed. "Could you send something for Patch too? He was ever so brave!"

"Of course," said Mr Periwinkle. "It was a big adventure for a little puppy. He was lucky to have you to look out for him."

"Woof!" said Patch.

As she walked past, Rosalind thought she saw Mr Periwinkle glance at the silver locket that hung around her neck. She turned back as she reached the front door, but he'd already walked away down the driveway to thank the

police officers once more.

She followed the others, her forehead creasing thoughtfully as she climbed up the stairs.

The princesses sat on Rosalind's bed eating delicious Chocorama Crunch biscuits. The famous cookies had layers of honeycomb and biscuit all joined together by toffee with a coating of thick chocolate all around the outside. Rosalind didn't think she'd ever tasted a biscuit so crunchy and sweet.

Patch had fallen asleep on the pillow. An uneaten doggie treat lay next to him and his little furry tummy rose and fell peacefully. Every now and then he twitched one floppy ear, as if he was having happy dreams.

"These are scrummy," said Isabella, taking another biscuit. "I have to take

some home to Belatina with me."

Lottie nodded, her mouth full. "Mmm . . . me too!"

Rosalind picked up the *Book of Ninja*. She touched the hard black cover and admired the gold lettering on the front.

"It's great that we've got the ninja book now," said Amina. "Just think how much we can learn! You must be really happy, Rosalind. You wanted to find it most of all."

Rosalind sighed. "We can't keep it though."

Lottie nearly swallowed the biscuit she was chewing. She coughed. "But . . . why?" she said at last. "You've been going on and on about finding it for ages."

"I know," said Rosalind. "But I saw Mr Periwinkle look at the locket just now when we came inside and I thought he recognised it. It made me realise that

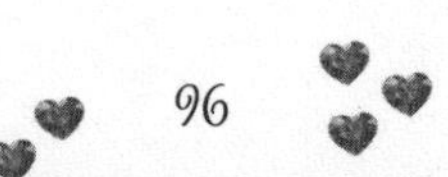

we can't keep the book or the locket. I mean – I know they were hidden. But the book was here, in this house. So it really belongs here. And the locket may have come from Taldonia too."

Amina nodded slowly. "I know what you mean. I wondered about that. We found the locket in my palace library, but someone must have taken it there. I'm sure it doesn't come from my country."

"So what shall we do?" said Isabella. "Do you want to put the book back in the clock tower?"

"No." Rosalind hugged the book fiercely. "I think we should take the book and the locket to Mr Periwinkle and tell him how we found them."

"You are a strange one, Rosy!" said Lottie. "First you can't think of anything except finding that book and now you've got it, you won't keep it."

Rosalind smiled and shook back her fair hair. "I just think it's what a Rescue Princess should do."

## Chapter Ten

# The Tale of the Book of Ninja

Rosalind went downstairs, holding the *Book of Ninja* in both hands. A heavy feeling filled her stomach and she knew it wasn't because of all the Chocorama Crunch biscuits she'd eaten. It was the thought of giving up the book. *We're doing the right thing*, she told herself. She tried not to look at Lottie, who was still glancing at the book and frowning.

"It'll be all right," Amina whispered to her. "We'll still be able to practise lots of

ninja moves together, even if we don't have the book!"

"Where will Mr Periwinkle be?" Isabella came downstairs carrying Patch, who had woken up now and was looking around with big brown eyes.

"Did you say you were looking for Mr Periwinkle, Your Majesty?" said a maid, who was passing by with a pile of sheets and towels. "He's in the little sitting room at the top of the stairs."

"Oh, thank you," said Isabella.

They headed back up the stairs and peeked round the door of the little room where they had first met Patch. The red and blue doggie bed was still there on the rug and a cheerful fire burned in the fireplace. Mr Periwinkle sat in an armchair, staring thoughtfully into the fire and holding a pile of glowing emeralds in one hand.

He saw them and smiled. "Come in, girls! Did you enjoy the biscuits?"

"They were delicious, thank you," said Isabella.

"Mr Periwinkle! We have something to tell you!" Rosalind burst out.

"Gracious!" said Mr Periwinkle. "Do come in!"

The girls crowded into the room and stood around Mr Periwinkle's chair, close to the roaring fire.

"It's all about this book," Rosalind told Mr Periwinkle. "I mean . . . I need to start at the beginning with the locket." She laid the *Book of Ninja* on the coffee table and took the silver locket from around her neck.

"This locket has a little key inside it." She opened it up to show him. "We found it on a bookshelf in the palace in Kamala where Amina lives. There was a special

BOOK OF
NINJA

message left beside it."

"I noticed your locket earlier. It looks just like one that my grandmother used to tell me about." Mr Periwinkle got up and took an old photo album down from the bookcase. "This was my grandmother when she was young." He showed the princesses a black and white photo of a smiling lady, wearing a locket on a chain around her neck.

Amina came over to look. "Wow! Her locket looks exactly the same. It has the bird with the open wings on the front."

"The land of the soaring eagle," muttered Rosalind.

"That's right!" said Mr Periwinkle. "Taldonia is known as the land of the soaring eagle. My grandmother told me all about her locket, but I never saw it. By the time I was born, she had already taken the locket far away and hidden it."

Rosalind's eyes widened. "But why did she hide it?"

"To save the eagles," said Mr Periwinkle. "For hundreds of years, golden eagles have built their nests high up at the top of the Pine Ridge Mountains. Their eggs are very precious. Thieves used to steal them and sell them for lots of money."

"That's awful!" cried Isabella.

"The eagles grew fiercer," continued Mr Periwinkle. "They swooped down on the egg robbers, pecking them with their sharp beaks and scratching them with their talons. That's when the thieves looked for a new way of stealing – a way to reach the nests without the birds seeing or hearing them."

"Ninja moves!" exclaimed Lottie.

Mr Periwinkle nodded. "They knew there was a special book in this house

that would give them the ninja ways they wanted. But my grandmother hid the book and took the clues for finding it far across the sea. She told me all this when I was a little boy. How I wished she hadn't hidden it. I wanted to try ninja moves too! But I was happy that the eagles were safe."

"So this must be the same locket. She must have hidden the locket and the key in my palace in Kamala!" said Amina. "It was there for years and years until we found it."

Mr Periwinkle leaned forwards eagerly. "I think it *is* the same one. But tell me! Where did you find the book?"

"It was hidden in the clock tower among the machinery of the clock. The little key opened the cupboard so that we could look inside," Lottie told him. "We decided to search in there because the

note said spend *time* looking and a clock tells the time."

"That sounds like my grandmother," chuckled Mr Periwinkle. "She loved riddles and clues."

"Now it makes sense that the note says: *'I have been moved to keep my secrets safe from those who would not use them wisely'*," cried Lottie. "Your grandmother was talking about the egg robbers. They were the ones who wouldn't have used it wisely."

Mr Periwinkle nodded. "They certainly didn't deserve the book's secrets."

"So that's how we found the book, but now we're giving it back," said Rosalind. "The book and the locket belong to you." She put the *Book of Ninja* and the locket in his hands.

Mr Periwinkle's brow creased. He looked through the book, smiling at some

of the pictures. "*How to Stay Hidden on a Mountainside,*" he read, and turned the page. "*Fifty Best Disguises*." He looked up at them. "Thank you for returning the silver locket, which I will keep to remember my grandmother. But the book belongs to you now. I think you may need it much more than me. Use it wisely!" He winked and handed the book back to Rosalind.

"But . . . but. . ." Rosalind turned pink, not knowing what to say.

"Thank you so much, sir!" Isabella curtsied. Patch woke up at the movement and barked indignantly.

"You'd better take these too." Mr Periwinkle passed the glowing emeralds to Isabella. "I have a feeling they must be yours. The policemen took them from one of the thieves."

Rosalind smiled and hugged the *Book*

*of Ninja*. "Thank you very much! I'm so happy we came to Taldonia."

"Ah, girls! There you are!" Rosalind's mum bustled into the room and Isabella quickly hid the bright emeralds behind her back. "You must go and get changed out of those muddy clothes. There's only an hour till the Autumn Ball begins."

"Can Patch come to the ball too?" Lottie picked up the puppy. "I'm sure he'd love to."

"He's a dear little thing, but rather grubby." Rosalind's mum wrinkled her nose as she looked at the dirt on Patch's coat. "Well, it's your ball, Albert. What do you think?"

"He really needs a bath to make him clean enough for the ball," said Mr Periwinkle. "In fact, it will be the first bath he's ever had."

Rosalind's blue eyes lit up. "Oh, do you

think . . . could *we* give him a bath?"

"Of course!" said Mr Periwinkle. "I can see how much you love him!"

"Just make sure you brush your hair and put your party clothes on first," said the Queen of Dalvia. "Then you can wear aprons so that you don't get water on your dresses."

The princesses rushed off to change.

"Lucky you, Patch!" said Amina. "You're getting your very first bath!"

## Chapter Eleven

# The Autumn Ball

Rosalind took the *Book of Ninja* carefully up to her room. She looked at a few more pages before hiding it under her pillow. She longed to get it out again and read every chapter.

There was a knock at the door. Lottie, Isabella and Amina stood outside wearing beautiful dresses and tiaras, and their shiniest party shoes.

"You haven't changed!" said Lottie. "You can't go to the Autumn Ball looking

like that!"

"Were you busy reading the book?" asked Amina.

Rosalind nodded. "If you wait a minute I'll get ready!" She pulled on her sky-blue party dress with its little cape to match. Then she put on her favourite gold tiara decorated with sparkling sapphires. She hurried out of her bedroom and shut the door.

Her friends were waiting for her in the corridor. Amina looked lovely in a long turquoise sari tied in a knot at one shoulder. Her tiara was made from arching loops of silver and her black hair hung loosely down her back.

"Is everyone ready then?" said Lottie, who was wearing a red dress covered with sparkling sequins. A beautiful golden crown dotted with rubies rested on her tight red curls.

Patch barked excitedly. "Patch is definitely ready!" said Isabella, picking him up and stroking him. Her yellow dress floated out as she moved and a swirly gold tiara gleamed on top of her brown hair.

"I bet you'll love being in the bath, won't you?" Rosalind said to Patch, rubbing his floppy ears.

The princesses took Patch to the bathroom, tied on their aprons and rolled up their sleeves. Amina turned the taps on and gradually the bathroom filled up with steam. When Rosalind put Patch into the water he wagged his tail madly. Then he barked at the taps, which were still gushing water.

"Good boy, Patch!" laughed Isabella. "You love the water, don't you?"

All the princesses had to hold Patch still so that they could wash him. They

rubbed dog shampoo into his coat and rinsed him thoroughly. When Rosalind got up to find a towel, he broke loose and scampered up the bath kicking his legs and covering the girls with water.

"Patch!" giggled Isabella. "There won't be any water left if you keep splashing like that!"

Rosalind found a big blue towel and wrapped him up in it. Then they lifted him out and took turns to dry him on the bath mat.

"That's so much better!" said Rosalind, admiring Patch's shiny coat.

"Woof!" said Patch, and broke away from the towel that kept tickling him. He bounded out of the bathroom and down the stairs. The princesses chased after him, giggling.

"Patch, come back!" laughed Rosalind.

"Woof, woof!" Patch galloped on,

thinking that this was a great new game. He got to the bottom of the stairs and skidded across the hallway.

"Oh, look! Isn't it beautiful!" said Amina.

The whole hallway had been hung with paper garlands and the ceiling twinkled with multicoloured lights. Music floated through the open doorway to the ballroom. Patch heard it too and pricked up his ears.

"No, Patch! Stop!" Rosalind dived towards him, but he scrambled out of her grasp and bounded right into the middle of all the kings and queens on the dance floor.

The royal guests stopped dancing to look in surprise at the excited puppy. The princesses stood in the doorway and Rosalind held her breath, hoping the grown-ups wouldn't get cross.

"And here are the brave princesses, who were determined not to leave a little puppy in danger," said Mr Periwinkle. "Come in and join the Autumn Ball!"

Rosalind, Amina, Lottie and Isabella quickly undid their aprons and hung them over the stairs before they went into the ballroom.

"Let's go and dance!" Rosalind grabbed Amina's hands and twirled her round. "Then tomorrow we can start learning moves from the *Book of Ninja*."

"It's so exciting!" said Isabella. "We can use the moves for our next adventure."

"Maybe we can teach some of them to Patch," grinned Lottie. "Wouldn't he make a great ninja dog?"

They all looked at Patch, who was galloping across the dance floor, and laughed.

Can't wait for
The Rescue Princesses's next
daring animal adventure?

# The Ice Diamond

Turn the page for
a sneaky peek!

## Chapter One

# The Little Snow Leopard

Princess Maya sprang up the mountainside, leaping over rough stones and clumps of little star-shaped flowers. She climbed and climbed until she reached the huge flat rock called Ching-May Peak. Clambering on to the stone, she pushed her long black plait over her shoulder and gazed all around.

"I can see for miles. The palace looks so tiny!" she told Deena.

"How did you climb up so fast?" puffed

the rosy-cheeked lady who was walking up to join her. "You're like a mountain goat!"

Deena was a groom at the palace and, as well as looking after the horses, she also looked after the King's wildlife projects.

Maya turned to look at the view again while she was waiting for Deena to catch up. The grey-turreted palace that she lived in had shrunk to the size of a toy castle. All around it were the streets and houses of the city and beyond that were the fields which swept up to the foot of the mountain.

"I love it up here," she said, smiling. "I'm so glad you let me come with you."

"I'm pleased to have the extra help. I'd like to make a full report of which wild animals we see to the King." Deena took out a notepad and pencil. "It's important

that he knows how well the wildlife project's going."

"Do you think we'll see any snow leopards up here?" asked Maya.

"I really hope so," Deena replied.

Everyone in the Kingdom of Lepari knew that the numbers of snow leopards had fallen over the last few years. It was worrying how few of them were left. The King, Maya's dad, had set up a nature project to help the endangered animals. It meant that no one was allowed to hurt them or to build houses on the mountain slopes where they lived. That way the creatures would be able to live in peace.

Maya tilted her head back to look at the top of the tallest mountain peak that glittered white with snow. A few weeks ago the whole mountainside had been white but now it was springtime again.

"There are two mountain sheep over

here," said Deena, scribbling on her notepad. "Can you see anything else, Maya?"

Maya turned her attention to the mountain slopes. Snow leopards were always well camouflaged. Their grey and white patterned coats were hard to see against the rocky mountainside but if she looked really carefully she knew she might spot one.

"Look! There's a snow leopard!" Maya pointed. "Right next to those bushes."

"Wonderful!" Deena smiled. "It's moving slowly. I wonder if it's hunting for food."

The beautiful leopard had thick white fur, speckled with dark rosettes. Maya watched it prowl across the mountain slope. It paused, crouching behind a boulder, its tail flicking from side to side.

"Some people still call them by their

old name: Spirit of the Mountain," said Deena softly. "I think it's because they're so graceful."

"It's amazing how they're such good climbers," said Maya.

Deena nodded. "This one's quite small so it's probably a girl. I wonder if it has any cubs.'

Maya looked round eagerly. "I'd love to see some cubs!"

Deena wrote on her notepad. "Keep looking then. Snow leopard dens are usually well hidden to keep the cubs safe."

Maya scanned the mountainside carefully. There! Something was moving among the rocks. It was small and white. "Deena!" Maya tugged at her sleeve. "Is that a snow leopard cub?"

The white shape moved, letting them see a small furry head. Deena smiled

broadly. "Yes it is! It's a good thing I brought you along, Maya. Your eyes are much sharper than mine."

The larger snow leopard gave a low growl and the cub bounded out from behind a rock. It gazed around at first, then jumped out and scampered across to its mother. Rubbing against her legs, it gave a little growl.

Maya's heart thumped. "It's so lovely," she whispered. "I wish we could go a bit closer."

"It's best not to disturb them," Deena reminded her.

The mother leopard padded further up the mountainside and the cub followed her, bounding playfully from rock to rock...